NATASHA THE BROWNIE

NATASHA THE BROWNIE

VERONICA HELEY

Illustrated by Annabel Large

Scripture Union
130 City Road, London EC1V 2NJ.

By the same author
Natasha's Badge
Natasha's Swing
For older readers:
Good for Kate!
Hawkeye of Paradise Row
The Paradise Row Gang
Sky High

First published 1990

ISBN 0 86201 625 8

Phototypeset by Input Typesetting Ltd, London
Printed and bound in Great Britain by Cox and Wyman Ltd, Reading

Contents

The talent show

There was to be a talent show in the church hall. Pod and Natasha were such great friends that they decided to do a 'Doctor, Doctor' sketch together, and they practised for weeks to get it just right. Natasha and Pod always meant well, but somehow they were always getting into bother. This time, however, everything was going to be perfect, and everyone would be proud of them.

Natasha's cousin Emmy was going to dance a solo, and her parents had hired a spangly costume for her to wear. As Natasha's mummy took the three children to the concert Emmy said, 'I'm sure to be the star of the show. My dancing teacher said I was a real little performer!'

'Grr!' said Natasha, softly, to Pod.

'Wham, splat!' said Pod back. Which made them

feel a lot better.

Natasha's mummy suddenly stopped and said, 'Oh, I forgot to post these letters. I'll go round by the post-box and meet you at the hall. Surely you can't get into any trouble between there and here. Natasha, drop these magazines into Mrs Dovey's on the way. She was due back from her daughter's last night, and may need something from the shops.'

Off she sent, and while Emmy waited on the pavement, Pod and Natasha turned into Mrs Dovey's gate. But Mrs Dovey didn't reply to their knock, and her curtains were still drawn.

'Hurry up!' cried Emmy. 'You know we won't be allowed to do our turns if we're not there at the start.'

Pod said, 'We could drop the magazines through the letter-box and call in later. Perhaps she's not back yet.'

'I can see a light on in the hall,' said Natasha, 'and I can hear something; maybe she's got the radio on.'

Emmy said, 'Perhaps it's a burglar. Look, I'm going on. I'm not going to risk losing my turn by being late, even if you are.'

Off she went. Pod and Natasha looked at one another. They desperately wanted to go, too, but somehow it just wasn't possible.

'There's someone crying in there,' said Pod. 'Suppose Mrs Dovey's got stuck. She's awfully old and her legs aren't very reliable.'

Pod and Natasha shouted through the letter-box and this time they both heard Mrs Dovey's voice, sounding very weak.

'I've broken my leg! Get the spare key . . . greenhouse!'

Pod and Natasha tore round the side of the house and wrestled the side door open to get into the back garden. What a mess! The grass hadn't been cut for ages, and just about everything you could think of had been dumped on it: plant pots, an old mattress, a broken chair. Beyond was a wreck of a greenhouse, with most of the glass missing.

'Wow!' said Pod, 'What a place for hide and seek!'

Natasha said, 'My dad offered to help her clear it up, but she doesn't like things being disturbed. I bet she fell down the stairs because the stair carpet is loose and she won't let anyone fix it.'

They clambered over the rubbish, and found an old wheelbarrow wedged across the door to the greenhouse. They tried to move it, but it wouldn't budge.

It looked dangerous to climb through a broken window, but they decided it had to be done. They piled enough flower pots together to make something to stand on, and then Natasha pushed, and

Pod heaved himself up . . . and dropped down inside.

The greenhouse was full of piles of newspaper, an old pram, and a jumble of garden tools.

'Where do we start looking?' said Pod in despair.

'Under flower pots,' suggested Natasha, trying to scramble up as well, but finding it rather hard on her hands and clothes.

'Got it!' shouted Pod. He thrust the key up through the broken window to Natasha. Then he had to get out again. He stood on the edge of the pram, and with Natasha pulling, he managed to hoist himself up and out again.

'Phew!' said Natasha, brushing dirt off her hands.

'Ouch!' said Pod, pushing his fingers through a tear in his trousers.

'Oh, well,' said Natasha, swallowing hard, 'We couldn't have got to the concert in time, anyway.'

'Doctor, doctor,' said Pod sadly. 'We need a doctor . . .'

They let themselves in through the front door, and there was Mrs Dovey, lying at the foot of the stairs. It was very cold in the house, but luckily she hadn't taken off her outdoor coat before she slipped and fell. She pointed to the phone, which was in the living-room. Pod dialled for an ambulance, while Natasha fought to light the gas stove and make a cup of tea, just as she sometimes did for her mummy.

The ambulance people told Pod to get some blankets off the bed and keep Mrs Dovey warm. Pod and Natasha did this, and sat with her till the ambulance came. The ambulance men carefully lifted Mrs Dovey into a wheelchair, and were just putting her into the ambulance when Natasha's Aunt Molly came running along the road to look for them.

'Pod! Natasha! Look at you! Oh, you naughty children, what have you been up to? Your mother asked me to come and find you. She's busy doing teas at the hall.'

One of the ambulance men said, 'Now don't you scold them, missus. Proper little heroes they were. Just about saved this lady's life, I reckon!'

'We're very sorry to have missed the concert,' said Pod and Natasha to Aunt Molly as they waved Mrs Dovey off. 'How did Emmy do?'

Aunt Molly looked as if she wanted to smile but didn't think she ought to do so.

'Well, she looked lovely of course, and she started all right, but then she tripped and tore her costume. After that she lost her temper, and didn't finish. Such a pity.'

'Ah,' said Natasha, not quite looking at Pod. She knew he'd be trying not to laugh, too.

They got to the hall as the concert finished, but Aunt Molly marched them on to the stage and told everyone why Pod and Natasha hadn't made it in time.

'And,' concluded Aunt Molly, '*we* were only offering our talents of singing and dancing and telling of stories to entertain you. But these two children were offering their own selves to Jesus, by giving up their chance to shine before an audience, and working to save Mrs Dovey. I think they must have pleased Jesus more than any of us today. So what I say is, three cheers for Pod and Natasha!'

'Oh,' said Natasha, 'How embarrassing!'

The Brownie

Cousin Emmy twirled to show off her brand new Brownie uniform, and said, 'Look at me!' She was wearing a yellow polo shirt and scarf, with brown culottes. Over the shirt she wore a sash.

Natasha's mummy was trying to place a badge on the sash, and said, 'Stand still, Emmy! Natasha, could you do the washing up for me while I do this?'

Natasha sighed, but started on the washing up. Somehow it was always her who got asked to do the washing up, and never Emmy. Life was very unfair at times.

Emmy said, 'I got this badge because of the dancing display, and I'm borrowing my father's stamp collection to show Brown Owl, so's I can get my Collector's badge. I'm going to have lots and lots of badges, more than anyone else in the whole world.'

'Fine,' said Natasha's mummy, 'and I'm sure Natasha will soon catch you up. She's coming along today for the first time, though of course she won't get her uniform till she joins officially.'

Natasha wasn't sure she wanted to join the Brownies. She'd hardly know anyone there, and if they were all like Emmy, it wasn't going to be much fun. Also, she knew Brownies have to keep themselves neat and tidy, and Natasha wasn't good at that.

The only reason she'd agreed to go was that Pod had joined the Beaver Colony which was run by Natasha's daddy, so he wouldn't be around to play with her, and there wasn't much else to do on a Monday night.

So along she went. She walked behind Emmy into the big hall and was introduced by Brown Owl to the other girls in her Six, who were the Pixies. Emmy was a Gnome. Natasha was pleased that she wasn't a Gnome, too. She felt it gave her a better chance, not being in the same Six as Emmy.

The other girls smiled at her, but didn't talk to her much. Natasha felt very much alone. It seemed as if they all had lots of badges.

But then it got better, for they started to play some fun games, and Natasha wasn't bad at games.

She forgot about being shy and really enjoyed herself, especially when her Six came out with top points. That was brill!

If only Emmy hadn't been there, it would have been almost perfect.

Then they made some peppermint creams, and that was absolutely perfect, and Natasha forgot all about Emmy for several minutes. But when she went to the toilet, Natasha overhead Emmy talking to one of the other Brownies.

'Oh, Natasha? She's my cousin. Her people aren't at all well off, you know. She's very untidy, and always getting into trouble. I feel sorry for you girls in her Six. She'll pull you right down.'

Natasha felt herself go bright red with shame. She didn't come out of the toilet until she was sure they'd gone.

She looked in the mirror. Emmy was quite right, she did look a mess. One ribbon was off, and the other untied. She had a smudge on her nose, her T-shirt was hanging out and her socks were at half mast.

She tried to put herself right, but washing only seemed to make the smudge worse, and when she pulled up her socks, one of them produced a hole.

Natasha would have burst into tears, if she'd been that sort of girl. But she wasn't. She was the

sort that soldiers on. But she was so miserable that she did have a little pray to Jesus.

'Please, Jesus, help me. I know I'm untidy, and always getting into trouble because of it. Help me get through the evening, without letting the others down!'

When she went back into the hall she thought she saw the others smiling and talking about her. She pretended she didn't care, but she did, really.

She was so unhappy that it took a real effort to join in with the others at singing time. She could hardly manage to croak through a chorus, even though it was one of her favourites.

She saw her Sixer go up to Brown Owl and say something, looking over at Natasha. Natasha just knew what they were saying, and she wanted to howl with shame. But she didn't. She kept on keeping on, trying to do her best to keep up with the others, and trying not to let them down.

At the end of the evening Natasha waited while some Brownies made arrangements about being tested for badges. Emmy came up, hugging her father's book of stamps. Brown Owl ignored Emmy to smile at Natasha, and ask if she'd enjoyed her first time with them.

'In bits,' said Natasha, 'but please, I won't be coming again. I know I've let the others down, being so untidy. I can't seem to help it. I'm sorry.'

'But, my dear,' said Brown Owl, 'you were just lovely. You helped the Pixies win the games and joined in everything. I know your Sixer is delighted to have you. As for being untidy, well, it's part of the Brownie training to deal with that. For instance, why don't you ask your mother if you can use toggles on your hair, instead of ribbons? I could never manage ribbons myself, when I was your age.'

'Oh,' said Natasha, 'that would be ace! But I don't know that I could ever manage to get any badges. I'm not clever, or anything.'

Brown Owl smiled. 'Well, Natasha, if you do decide to join us, I don't think that would be too much of a problem. Your Aunt Molly is a friend of mine and she's always telling me the nice things you do to help other people. She says you've been helping your mummy ever such a lot with the housework and that means you can work towards the House Orderly badge straight away. Didn't you take part in a play at school last term? That would count towards the Jester badge. And I believe you made a collection of sea shells when you were on holiday, and looked them up in a book, and named them. Bring it to show me some time, and we'll see what else you need to do for the Collector badge.'

'Oh!' said Natasha. 'Really! All those badges for me?'

'You put your talents to work, and you get something to show for it, just as the people did in the Bible. Do you remember? Those who put their talents to work were well and truly rewarded, and the one who didn't, got into a lot of trouble. You don't have to be brilliant at maths or have lots of money to get on, but you do have to make the most of what you've got. Right?'

'Right!' said Natasha.

Brown Owl turned to Emmy and looked through her father's book of stamps. 'I'm sorry, Emmy, but this isn't your collection, is it? I'm afraid I can't start you off on the Collector badge, until you bring me a collection that you've made yourself.'

Emmy was furious, but had to accept what Brown Owl said. Natasha waited for her daddy and Pod, who were coming to collect her after they'd tidied up at Beavers. Pod came out first and said, 'Guess what, Beavers is just ace!'

And Natasha said, 'Guess what! Brownies is brill, too!'

Jericho

Pod had very few toys, and his most treasured possession was his little cat, Jericho. He and his mother lived in a flat above some shops, just down the road from Natasha. Pod's father was away working on an oil rig up north, but when he'd been with them at Christmas, he'd made a cat flap in the back door, so that Jericho could go in and out as he pleased.

Sometimes Natasha and Pod would play hide and seek at the back of the flats, up and down the fire escapes, and round the dustbins and through the overgrown alley. Jericho could hide better than they did, and he always found them when they hid.

But one awful day Jericho refused to come down the fire escape to play. He was shivering. Then he sneezed, and went on sneezing.

Pod and Emmy were having tea at Natasha's house that day. Pod said, making a joke of it, 'Guess what! Jericho's caught a cold!'

Emmy said, 'Silly! Cats can't catch cold.'

Natasha's mummy said, 'I'm afraid they can, Emmy. There is such a thing as cat flu, you know. Perhaps Jericho ought to see the vet. Has he had his flu injection, do you know?'

Pod looked as if he were going to cry. 'I didn't know cats had to have injections. Jericho will be all right, won't he?'

Emmy said, 'He'll probably die.'

Pod rushed from the tea table and hid in the back garden. Natasha found him there, and gave him some biscuits she'd saved from her own tea.

'Perhaps,' said Natasha, 'you could ask your mummy to take him to the vet when she gets back from work tonight.'

When Pod's mummy got back from work, she did take Jericho to the vet, and he told her how to look after him. The vet said Jericho was a very young cat, and seemed to be very poorly, but time would tell.

Pod wasn't sure what that meant, but he saw that his mother looked upset so he gave Jericho an extra cuddle before he went to bed. The next day Jericho wasn't any better, and Pod could hardly wait to get back from school to see how he was.

Natasha went with him. Jericho was curled up in a little ball in his basket and would hardly open his eyes. He did try to purr when Pod stroked him but he hadn't eaten any food that day, or taken any milk.

Pod and Natasha sat with him, silently, hoping for the best. But next morning Jericho wasn't in his basket when Pod went to look.

Pod's mummy sat him on her knee, and said, 'Poor little Jericho. He was feeling so poorly, and now he has gone away from us to get better.'

'I don't understand,' said Pod. 'Where is he?'

'He went to sleep in the night, and didn't wake up this morning. I've put him in a shoe box, out of sight.'

Pod couldn't bear it. He didn't cry, but he wouldn't speak all that day at school. He didn't eat his lunch, either, but just sat there, making Natasha feel guilty for eating hers. She felt like crying, too. She'd loved Jericho almost as much as Pod. It was an awfully long day. Pod tried to excuse himself from going home with Natasha for tea, but Natasha made him come. She felt this was a job for her mummy.

'Listen, Pod,' said her mummy, taking him on her knee. 'This world isn't always perfect. Bad things happen, and sad things happen; like your father having to be away so much, and people and animals dying before we're ready to let them go.'

'You don't understand!' cried Pod. 'It was all my fault. I ought to have known about the flu injections, and done something about it, and then Jericho wouldn't have died!'

'Now you don't know that, and you mustn't blame yourself. It wasn't up to you to think of cat injections. I blame myself a bit. I did know, and I ought to have checked.'

Pod said, 'I can't bear to think of him being gone for ever and ever. At school today Emmy said cats don't ever go to heaven, and I'll never see him again.'

'God made all living creatures,' said Natasha's mummy. 'He knows and cares about even the smallest of sparrows, so of course he knows all about Jericho, who was a lot bigger than a sparrow.'

'Jericho used to catch and eat sparrows,' said Pod. 'I used to tell him not to, but he would do it. Do you suppose Jesus minded?'

'Sparrows were food for him. That was the way he was made. Look to Jesus for comfort, and he will give it to you. Now I suggest that you give Jericho a proper burial in the garden. We'll all come and sing a hymn and pray a bit, and lay him to rest in one of the places where he used to play hide and seek.'

Everyone came to the funeral: Pod's mummy, Aunt Molly and her husband, and Natasha's daddy and mummy. At the last minute Emmy arrived, wearing a black lace scarf over her hair and carrying a beautiful bunch of flowers from the florist's shop. Pod and Natasha were surprised to see Emmy, and even more surprised when she acted just as she should.

They sang 'All things bright and beautiful, All creatures great and small,' and Pod lowered the box containing Jericho into a hole that Natasha's daddy had dug under a flowering bush.

Then Natasha gave a short speech saying what a clever, pretty cat Jericho had been, and how he'd lived life to the full, having to be rescued from trees by firemen, and frightening the lives out of them when he made them think he was a werewolf, and that he'd been the terror of all the sparrows, and they would all miss him a lot.

Natasha's mummy said a prayer thanking Jesus for all the fun they'd had with Jericho, and then they all said the Lord's Prayer, because it felt right. Pod's mummy said something long and complicated in Polish, Pod threw in some earth, and Natasha's daddy filled in the hole.

Then they all went into the house to have a funeral feast of lemonade and cake.

Emmy said, 'That was nice. I had a hamster,

once. It was the prettiest thing, and so soft, you wouldn't believe. It died, and my daddy threw it away in the rubbish. I cried. I really liked that hamster.'

Pod and Natasha looked at Emmy. Perhaps she really was human, after all!

The craft fair

Cousin Emmy boasted, 'We're going to make the most money in the whole world!'

They were preparing for the craft fair, which brought in a lot of money for the church. Everyone was busy making things. Then they would rent a table at the fair and sell what they'd made.

You never saw such beautiful things; there were hand-made sweaters and children's clothes, furry toys, jams and marmalades and pickles, and all kinds of home-made cakes and biscuits.

There were pots and vases and pretty things to hang in windows. There was one stall which sold nothing but furniture and fittings for dolls' houses.

Emmy's parents had booked a stall. They had bought a large quantity of silk flowers cheaply, and proposed to sell them at a profit. Emmy said theirs would be the stall that made the most money at the fair.

Natasha's mummy said, 'What are you going to do at the fair, Natasha?'

Natasha shrugged. She looked at Pod, and he shrugged, too. They couldn't make things to sell. They weren't clever enough, or old enough for that.

Natasha said, 'We'd like to help. Brown Owl did say there would be a way we could help, but I don't know what it is.'

'The Beavers are helping, too,' said Pod, 'because we've been told to wear our uniforms on Saturday.'

'So have the Brownies,' said Natasha.

Emmy said, 'Huh! What can you lot do to help! Not much, I should think. I feel sorry for you. Brown Owl did ask me to help her, but I've something better to do! I'm wearing a new white dress, and I'm going to have a wreath of silk flowers in my hair, and I'm going to help sell the flowers. That's what I call worthwhile helping.'

Natasha and Pod were afraid she was right, but they'd promised, so on Saturday they put on their uniforms and went along to help.

Natasha's daddy was on the door, taking entrance money. He made a big point of letting Natasha and Pod through with the other helpers.

Natasha's mummy went off to help in the kitchens, while Natasha and Pod looked for their leaders. The hall and all the other rooms were filled with big tables, with lots of exciting things on them – puppets and dolls, sweets in every colour and shape. It was hard to keep your eyes off them, and your money in your pocket.

Pod was whisked off by another Beaver, and Natasha found Brown Owl in the room next to the kitchen.

Brown Owl was rushed off her feet. 'I'm glad you've come early, Natasha. We've so much to do. Some of the Brownies are taking teas and coffees round to the stallholders, but we have to make up ploughman's lunches to sell later. We put some of each on a plate, with some salad, and cover it over with clingfilm. Could you help me by cutting up the bread?'

'Is this about right?' said Natasha, cutting away with care.

'Splendid! And here come some more Brownies to help. Isn't Emmy coming, too?'

'She's on a stall already.'

'Oh, well . . . I expect we can manage.'

Natasha cut bread till her forefinger was sore and her arm ached. Another Brownie came to help her. Two more Brownies cut up cheese and butter, while others washed and cut up salad and one filled little pots with chutneys. More Brownies kept coming and going, taking trays with cups of coffee and tea out, and bringing back the empties.

'Phew!' said Natasha, piling the last bits of bread on plates. 'What a marathon that was!'

'Well done!' said Brown Owl. 'Now you can have some orange squash and a biscuit, free. You've worked very hard, and deserve a break. Go and look round all the stalls, but be back in half an hour, when we start to serve lunches.'

Natasha went looking for Pod. There were masses of people at the fair, all talking and buying, and having a good time. There were so many people, it was hard to get round. The stallholders seemed happy, too.

Natasha's daddy was just finishing his stint on the door, and her mummy was sitting with her feet up, having a well-earned cuppa. She had asked a stallholder to put aside a lovely cherry red jumper for Natasha to wear that winter. Natasha was thrilled with the jumper. It was soft and cuddly and had a big black and white panda worked into the front. It was ace.

She hung over the dolls' furniture for a bit because it was so pretty you could just look at it for ever, but she wasn't really a doll person, so she bought some home-made fudge and biscuits at the next stall, to share with her mummy and daddy and with Pod.

But where was Pod? She hadn't seen him anywhere.

She found Emmy's stall, though. It was a picture, with a framework of silk flowers over it. But Emmy herself didn't look happy.

It was most unfortunate, but next door to Emmy's stall was one selling real live flowers, beautifully arranged, and people all seemed to prefer them. Emmy's parents didn't look happy, either. They had sold enough to cover their costs, but not much more.

'Ouch!' Natasha was hit in the back. There was Pod, grinning. He and a Beaver friend were going around with a big plastic bag, picking up all the litter that people dropped. It was the Beavers' task to keep the place tidy, and they were doing a brilliant job.

Then it was time for Natasha and a Brownie friend to help serve the lunches. To and fro they went, offering their ploughman's lunches to the stallholders and to the people who had come to the fair, helping people to chutneys and knives and forks, and taking orders for tea and coffee at the same time.

It was hard to keep track of all the different things that people wanted, so Natasha took the orders down on a piece of paper, while another Brownie collected the money.

They were so busy Natasha didn't notice how

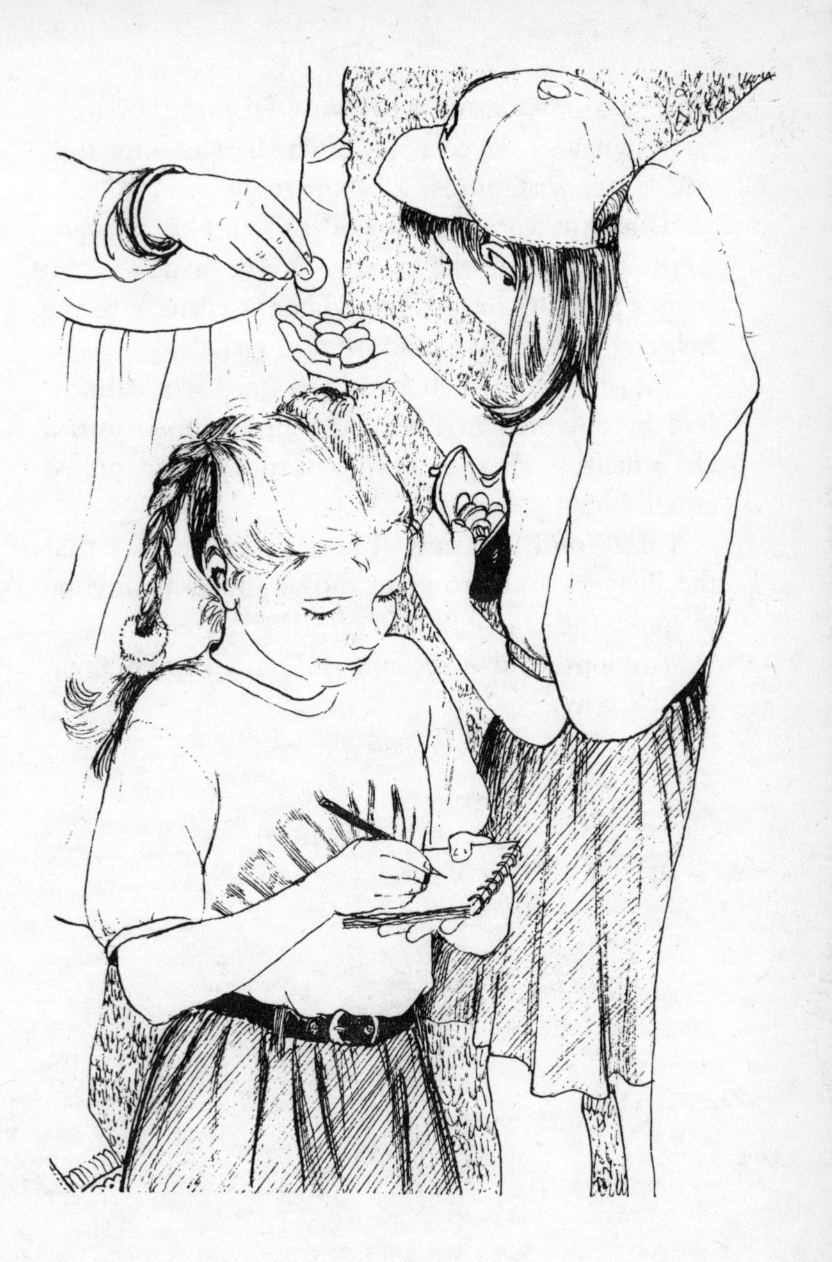

time was passing until Brown Owl said they must sit down and have some lunch. It was only then she saw it was almost time for tea!

'That was very good,' said Brown Owl, smiling as she counted up the money. 'We've made an even bigger profit than last year. Thanks entirely to my helpers! I'm really proud of you, girls!'

Natasha beamed. It had been hard work, but it had been worth it. Pod came and flopped into a chair nearby. He was worn out, too. But he looked equally happy.

'I feel good!' he said. 'I heard someone say that the Beavers and Brownies did as much as anyone to make the craft fair a success!'

'You put yourselves into it,' said Brown Owl. 'That's why.'

The treasure hunt

Natasha's mummy said, 'You remember Mrs Dovey?'

''Course I do,' said Natasha. 'Pod and I helped get her into hospital when she broke her leg.'

'She's decided not to go back to her house, but to live with her daughter instead. Her daughter lives a long way off so Mrs Dovey's asked me to fetch some things that she wants to keep from the old house. Then it can be cleared and put up for sale.'

'Can we help?' asked Natasha.

'Of course. I'll be glad of help, because Mrs Dovey says she's hidden her treasures in different places all over the house, for fear of burglars. The only problem is, she can't remember exactly where she's put everything.'

‘Wowee!’ said Pod. ‘A real live treasure hunt!’

So on Saturday they put on their oldest clothes and went into the empty house.

Even going into that house was an adventure, because it was a Perilous Place to be in. Natasha put her foot through a rotten floorboard, and her leg disappeared, right up to her knee! Luckily she wasn’t hurt.

Pod found a waterfall upstairs, where a leaking tap had caused a washbasin to overflow, and the door came off the cupboard under the stairs when Natasha’s daddy went there to turn off the water and the electricity.

Natasha said, ‘This is more exciting than anything!’

Pod said, ‘Do you think there are any wild animals lurking, ready to pounce on us?’

Natasha’s daddy ripped up the remains of the stair carpet, so that no-one else could trip and break their leg on it, and they started to search.

Mrs Dovey had given them a list of things she wanted and they soon found three bundles of silver cutlery, and a pearl necklace. But nothing else was where it ought to be!

Pod found a silver tray under the mattress in the spare room, and Natasha cried ‘Eureka! More treasure!’ when she discovered the silver teapot wrapped in newspaper behind the screen in the fireplace.

Meanwhile Natasha's mummy and daddy collected Mrs Dovey's photograph albums, and the pretty porcelain figures from the sitting-room mantelpiece, and packed up all her clothes.

'Bang, bang!' cried Natasha, peering through a grubby bedroom window. 'Take cover, Pod! There's a wild animal lurking in the jungle outside!'

Pod said, 'Why, it's a cat!' He forced the window open, and called out, 'Here, pussy, pussy!'

The cat darted off, disappearing inside the broken greenhouse.

Pod said, 'Do you think the cat is lost treasure, too?'

Natasha's mummy said, 'If it's grey, it's Mrs Dovey's cat. A neighbour has been feeding it while she's in hospital. But the cat's very unhappy and has been neglecting itself, so the Cat Lady is coming to take it away.'

Pod said, 'What will the Cat Lady do to it?'

'She takes in unwanted cats, and finds new homes for them. Have you found Mrs Dovey's black tin box yet? We can't go till we've found it, because it contains all her private papers.'

But Pod had lost interest in the treasure hunt. He tore out into the back garden, miaowing to the cat.

At first the cat was afraid of him, but Pod was

good with animals, and soon it was purring round his legs. It was a pretty little cat, but it was rather thin and dusty-looking. It was grey all over except for a white chest and paws.

Pod stroked its fur. 'Poor pussy. You're so thin! And you feel so dirty!'

'I expect he's missing Mrs Dovey,' said Natasha. 'I wish we could do something for him.'

'There's plenty of tinned food left out for him, and milk,' said Pod, 'but he doesn't seem to want it.'

'I know what we can do for him!' said Natasha. 'We can give him a shower!'

There was an old watering-can nearby, half full of water. Before Pod could stop her, Natasha had emptied it over the cat! The poor cat didn't like it at all and darted under a tangle of bramble bushes, shivering and crying.

Pod said, 'Oh, come back, pussy!' and tried to scramble after him.

Natasha pulled him back. 'Pod, you'll hurt yourself!'

'What on earth are you doing?' The children turned round to see a nice-looking lady in a sweater and jeans, carrying a cat basket.

'The cat ran away,' said Natasha. 'He was all dirty, so I gave him a shower, but he didn't like

it.'

'I'm afraid it was the wrong thing to do,' said the Cat Lady. 'Cats hate water. Here, kitty . . .'

She put down a bowl full of delicious, freshly cooked fish, and the cat came crawling out on its tummy, and started to sniff at the food. The Cat Lady knelt down and rubbed the cat dry with a towel.

'Oh, let me do that,' said Pod. 'I know he won't mind me. I had a kitten once myself, but he died.'

Natasha said, 'It was my idea to wash it, not Pod's. I'm sorry. I didn't know.'

Pod said, 'If no-one else wants this cat, could I have him?'

The Cat Lady said, 'Let's ask your mummy, shall we? I'd need to know that he would be properly looked after, and given his injections.'

'We know all about that now,' said Pod. 'My mum won't mind. She misses our kitten. She said so only last night.'

'Then I'll have a talk with her, and see what she says. But you must remember that a cat like this, who's been left to run wild, may not want to become a house cat again. He may try to run away, back to this garden.'

'Well, we'd know where to find him, wouldn't we?'

Natasha's daddy gave Mrs Pod's telephone

number to the Cat Lady, who went off to find the phone.

Natasha's daddy said they'd found the tin box of papers in the fridge, and that was the lot. He looked up at the house, and shook his head. 'The house is not going to fetch much. It needs such a lot doing to it. A pity. It's a nice house, underneath.'

The Cat Lady came back and said Pod's mummy was delighted about the cat, and they could have it as soon as it had been checked over by the vet.

'How much money do you want for it?' said Pod. 'You can have everything I've got, only I'm afraid that's not very much.'

'I've got nearly a whole pound that you can have,' said Natasha, 'and I really am sorry about giving it a shower.'

'I don't want anything,' said the Cat Lady. 'I'm just doing God's work, looking after lost animals for him. What will you call him?'

'He has a name already,' said Natasha's mummy. 'He's called Silver because of his silvery-grey coat.'

'What a funny thing,' said Pod. 'We were hunting for silver when we found him.'

Mum's Day

'I've got a problem,' said Pod.

Natasha didn't stop skipping. 'Twenty-one, twenty-two . . . is it your new kitten, Silver?'

'No, he's fine.'

'Twenty-seven, twenty-eight . . . is it your dad?'

Natasha got her skipping rope tangled round her legs. Of course Pod was missing his dad, who hadn't been home for ages. If only he wasn't working so far away! Natasha tried to imagine what it would be like if her dad had to work so far away, and decided it didn't bear thinking about.

'It's not dad. It's my mum.'

'What about your mum? She's all right, isn't she?'

'It's Mothering Sunday coming up. I've made her a card and I want to give her a present, but I haven't got any money. I've thought till I'm tired, and I still can't think how to get her a present.'

'I haven't got a present for my mum, either. This calls for a Confabulation.'

Natasha liked big words. She saved them up for special occasions, when they might come in handy. Pod looked impressed when she used her new word, so she explained it meant a discussion, and they sat down under a tree in the playground to talk it over.

Natasha said, 'I made my mum a card, too. Only it went a bit wrong. My writing went so big I had to put 'Mum's Day' on it, instead of Mothering Sunday. I don't think she'll mind. I wanted to make her a nice present, too. I tried to make a plant pot holder with string, but it broke.'

'I tried to get some money, washing cars. But they said I was too little.'

'Cousin Emmy's buying her mother a bottle of scent, the new one that's on the telly adverts. She gets so much pocket money, she can easily afford it.'

'Yuk,' said Pod.

'Absolutely yuk,' said Natasha. 'Wow! I've just had an idea. You know our teacher was telling us about a special cake for Mothering Sunday? Girls who worked away from home used to take a simnel cake to their mothers when they went back to see them at this time of year. The teacher said some people believed the cake was called after a boy called Sim and a girl called Nell. Just like you and me, only different names.'

'That's right,' said Pod. 'Sim and Nell had an argument about whether the cake should be boiled or baked. So they did both, and named it after both of them, Sim-Nel cake. So what!'

'So why don't we make our mums a simnel cake?'

'Wouldn't it be too hard?'

'I've done some cooking at Brownies, and you're good at measuring. I bet we could do it, if we tried. What I think is, that we get permission for you and Silver to stay with us on Saturday night. We get up early on Mothering Sunday, and do it in our kitchen. Then it will be a lovely surprise for them.'

'You're on!' said Pod.

Their mothers agreed to Pod and Silver staying the night at Natasha's, so the first part of their plan went off very well.

Early on Sunday morning Pod and Natasha got out of bed and crept downstairs.

Pod had got properly dressed even though it was so early. While he fed Silver, Natasha tied a big apron of her mum's over her pyjamas and pushed her hair into her Brownie hat to keep it out of the way.

First they got down the big cookery book from

the shelf. Pod read off the list of things they needed while Natasha got them from the larder. They found everything except the marzipan, so they decided to do without that.

Pod rolled up his sleeves and measured everything out onto the table in piles. Natasha put the oven on to warm, found the baking tin, and started to crack eggs into a bowl.

Then disaster struck. Silver jumped up onto the table and accidentally knocked over half a bottle of milk. The milk went all over the table and got mixed up with the flour and the sugar and the currants.

'Mop it up, quickly!' shrieked Natasha.

'Can't you see I'm trying to hold it back with my hands?' shouted Pod. 'Get a cloth!'

'I can't! I'm cracking eggs . . .'

'It's going over the edge of the table . . .'

'Ouch! It's going down my tummy!'

Natasha hopped around, holding an egg in each hand, with the milk trickling down her pyjamas. Poor Silver was so alarmed at what he'd done that he dived off the table under Natasha's feet.

Pod shouted 'Look out!' but Natasha slipped and fell, bringing down the towel rail and knocking over the stack of pots and pans in the corner.

When the noise had died down, they remembered the grown-ups, and looked up at the ceiling.

Surely Natasha's father and mother must have heard them!

Nothing happened.

'It's all right,' whispered Natasha. 'I bumped myself really hard, but I didn't break the eggs!'

'Great!' whispered Pod back. 'And no-one heard us!'

And at that very moment Natasha's daddy walked in, pulling on his dressing-gown. 'What's going on here?' he said, and groaned when he saw the mess.

'Sorry,' said Natasha. 'We'll clean it up, honest. We were making a surprise present for mum . . .'

'A simnel cake,' said Pod. 'Only it got a bit complicated.'

'I can see that!' said Natasha's daddy. 'Well, if it's for Mothering Sunday, perhaps I'd better lend a hand.'

So Natasha's daddy showed them how to use the electric mixer which made cooking easy.

He said simnel cakes had to have marzipan, which was what made them different from other fruit cakes. So he looked up the recipe and helped them to make their own.

Then Pod spooned half the cake mixture into the baking tin, Natasha's daddy put in a layer of marzipan, and Natasha dolloped on the rest of the mixture, smoothing it off to go in the oven.

While the cake was baking, Pod and Natasha made twelve little balls of marzipan to go round the top of the cake – to remind them of the twelve apostles – and Natasha's daddy found some miniature sugar eggs to go in the middle, to show that Easter was coming.

Natasha's mummy came down before they had time to clean up the kitchen and she was a bit upset about the mess at first. But when she saw the cake she was thrilled, and agreed that of course you couldn't cook a surprise cake without making a mess. They cut the cake in two, and Natasha's mummy found a cake box for Pod to take half back home.

As for Pod's mummy, she said Pod had given her not one but two gifts for Mothering Sunday, the best cake she had ever tasted, and a Good Rest!

The Easter egg

Cousin Emmy took the last chocolate biscuit and said, 'What are you getting for Easter?'

'Getting?' said Natasha, puzzled. 'You mean presents? It's not Christmas or birthday.'

Natasha's mummy found another chocolate biscuit each for Pod and Natasha, and said, 'It's better than Christmas. Without Easter, we wouldn't have anything to be joyful about.'

Pod said, 'Mega-thanks for the biscuit.'

Emmy said, 'I'm getting my hair done, and a new dress, and of course the biggest Easter egg you ever did see.'

Pod and Natasha weren't interested in hair-dos or new clothes, but their eyes did shine at the thought of Easter eggs.

Natasha's mummy said, 'Yes, you will have one

each, though I don't think they'll be very big, because we're having so many people to lunch that day. Aunt Molly and Uncle Tom, and your old friend the Stilt Man, who works for children's charities, and . . .'

'And me and Mum?' enquired Pod. 'I did hope we'd go up north to be with Dad for Easter, but Mum says we have to stay here.'

'Of course you're coming,' said Natasha's mummy. 'And perhaps Emmy as well.'

'I should think not!' said Emmy. 'We're all flying to Tenerife for Easter.'

Pod and Natasha knew that Emmy's ideas of going away with her parents didn't always work out. They hoped she would go. They also hoped they'd be nice to her if she didn't. It put a strain on them, being nice to Emmy.

When Emmy had gone home, Natasha asked her mummy if she could have a chocolate egg with buttons in it, as this was her favourite.

'I hadn't forgotten,' said her mummy.

'And Pod?'

'I'll check with his mum and make sure he gets one. And Natasha, try to be kind to Emmy.'

'I do *try*,' said Natasha.

'I must warn you that Emmy's parents probably won't be taking her away with them. I expect they'll spend a great deal of money on presents for her instead.'

'You mean she really is getting a giant Easter egg?'

'Yes. Let's hope she remembers why we have eggs at Easter time. You remember why, don't you Natasha?'

Natasha nodded, though she didn't, not really. It was just something nice that happened at Easter time, like decorating the church with daffodils and all the other yellow flowers they could find, and singing really happy hymns that made you want to clap your hands.

She liked everything about Easter, and even managed to keep smiling when she heard that Emmy would not be going to Tenerife, and would be staying with them, instead. Natasha succeeded in being nice to Emmy right up to Easter morning when Pod rushed round before church to show them his very own chocolate egg. Natasha showed him hers, and everything was lovely until Emmy unpacked the one her parents had left for her.

Emmy's egg was so big she could hardly see over it! It made Pod and Natasha's normal-sized eggs look tiny. Pod and Natasha said, politely, how beautiful Emmy's egg was, and would she like to taste a piece of theirs.

Emmy accepted the pieces they offered her, and said, 'Don't you think this is the biggest and the best Easter egg there ever was? I'd rather have this than go to Tenerife. Don't you think it's super, Natasha?'

'Marvellous,' said Natasha, being generous about it. It did look marvellous, too. There were flowers on it, and fluffly nylon chickens and an enormous bow of yellow ribbon. Natasha thought there was enough chocolate in it for a whole family.

Emmy said, 'Don't you think it's splendid, Pod?'

'Wow!' said Pod, impressed. 'Can we have a bit of yours now?'

Emmy shook her newly-permed head. 'It's not for you. It's for me. All for me.'

The injustice of this bit deep into Natasha and Pod. They looked round for a grown-up to even things up, but all the grown-ups were either in the kitchen, or getting ready to go to church.

'Bother her!' said Pod to Natasha as they walked along.

'Hope it makes her sick!' said Natasha to Pod. And they continued to feel cross till they got to church.

It was lovely at church, with flowers and everyone being happy and having so much to celebrate. Pod and Natasha even managed to overlook the fact that Emmy had brought her egg to church for the other children to admire. Easter was too special to waste time on being jealous of other people's eggs.

The minister told all the children to come up to collect a chocolate egg from a big basket. He explained that eggs were the sign of new life, to remind us of the new life that started on the first Easter day when Jesus rose from the dead. He said an egg was also the symbol of the stone which had been rolled away from the empty tomb. All the children took an egg, and then they had to roll them down the aisle to see who reached the door first.

Off they went, rolling the eggs along. The eggs went all over the place, and the grown-ups started laughing. Everyone was laughing and happy, and Pod was the happiest of all when he got his egg to the door first, and was given an extra Easter egg as a prize.

Everyone thought it was a splendid way of remembering what happened on the morning when Jesus rose from the dead.

Even then the children didn't go straight back to their seats, but crowded round the minister as he showed them the Easter garden which Natasha's class had made, with the tomb all empty, and lit up with a pocket torch from inside. They sang Allelulias and clapped in time to the music, and only then did they go back to their seats for the final blessing.

But Natasha noticed that Emmy went bright red during the last prayer, and looked as if she were going to cry.

Emmy had accidentally sat down on her beautiful Easter egg and mashed it into dozens of pieces, which clung to her new dress when she stood up again.

Poor Emmy. Everyone made a fuss over her, and took her away to be cleaned up.

Pod said to Natasha, 'That's odd. If you'd told me it was going to happen, I'd have thought that I'd have laughed myself silly. But somehow, I don't want to laugh, now.'

'We've got friends and lots of people who like us,' said Natasha. 'She only had her egg.'

Pod said. 'Shall I give her the one I got for a prize?'

'She doesn't deserve it.'

'I know that,' said Pod. But he gave it to her, all the same.

Great Pa, ta

Easter had come and gone. One day more and they would be back at school. At church on Sunday Pod slumped in the pew, and refused to take part in the service. He wouldn't stand up to sing the hymns, he wouldn't put his hands together and bow his head when it came to prayers, and he kicked the front of the pew all through the minister's talk to the children.

After church Natasha asked Pod what was the matter.

Pod kicked the floor, and didn't reply.

'Is it your dad! Has something happened?'

Pod shook his head. 'I thought he'd be coming down to visit us for Easter, since we couldn't go up there. I thought it would be a nice surprise, like it was at Christmas. I haven't seen him since

Christmas.'

Natasha said, 'We could have a special pray about it.'

'It's no good. Do you think I haven't been praying, all this time? And that silly minister, going on about how much we've got to be thankful for, and telling us to make up our own prayers, like "Great Pa, ta!" '

Natasha said, 'But I liked that. It was, well, friendly. It made me feel closer to him.'

Pod hunched his shoulders. 'It was yuk. It made me feel sick.'

The minister had been comparing the lives of most children in Britain with those of the starving children in certain parts of Africa. Pod knew why the minister had told them to be thankful, but he just couldn't do it.

He was feeling sick at heart, just as sick as those poor children were, though in a different way.

'I'll tell you what I think,' said Pod. 'I've had enough of church and praying. It doesn't work. I'm not coming any more.'

Natasha went pale. She couldn't imagine coming to church without Pod. It would be awful. As she watched Pod trudge off all by himself, she heard the rustle of Cousin Emmy's new dress.

'Well!' said Cousin Emmy. 'Didn't Pod behave badly in church! Everyone's talking about it.'

Natasha felt like crying. 'He's upset about his dad not coming home at Easter.'

'I expect they're having a divorce,' said Cousin Emmy, casually. 'That's what happens, when people live apart. My mother and father have talked about it quite a lot.'

Natasha was shocked. 'But Emmy, that's awful! Aren't you upset?'

Emmy shrugged. 'So I get two homes and two lots of presents at Christmas and birthdays. So what?'

Natasha went to find her mummy and tell her what Emmy had said. 'Pod's father and mother aren't going to get a divorce, are they? I think he'd die if they did.'

'Oh, my dear, no! Of course not! Mr Pod couldn't get down for Easter because . . . well, there was a special reason, and you'll know all about it soon enough.'

'But Emmy said . . .'

'That's an entirely different matter. Emmy's parents are going through a rough time, and we must all pray for them.'

'I'm not praying for Emmy. She doesn't mind if they do get a divorce.'

'Emmy puts a brave face on it, but I'm sure she's very upset inside.'

Natasha wasn't so sure about that, but for the

moment she was more concerned about Pod.

'Pod says he's stopped praying, and won't come to church any more. I don't know what to do. I don't want to come to church either, if he doesn't!'

'Darling, you're not thinking straight. You believe Jesus loves you? And Pod? Remember that Jesus knows what's best for you and he loves you very much. He doesn't promise that everything will turn out exactly as you want it to in this world. But in this case . . . well, I wouldn't give up hope, and that's all I can say for the moment.'

'I'm fed up with secrets, and so is Pod. Every time he asks his mum about his dad, she gets cross and says she'll tell him when there's any news.'

Natasha's mummy sighed. 'Yes, it's very trying, waiting . . . but we've all got to be patient.'

That night Natasha had a nightmare about Pod's father getting in a boat and going away for good. She woke up crying, and was inclined to be cross with everyone next day. To make matters worse, Pod wouldn't talk to her, or answer when the teacher spoke to him. He even refused to play at break-time.

Natasha was afraid he'd get into serious trouble if he went on like that, so she dragged him aside into the corner under the beech tree.

He wouldn't even look at her, so she put her hands on her hips and said, 'Pod, you can't stop hoping. I won't let you! Let's have a pray about it, here and now. If it doesn't bring your dad back, at least it will make us feel better!'

'Won't!' said Pod.

'Then I will, and I shall hang on to you, so that you can feel my prayer, even if you're too stupid to pray for yourself!'

She shut her eyes tight, and prayed as hard as she could. She could feel Pod trying to pull away from her, but she didn't let go, and went on praying.

When she stopped and opened her eyes, he was still looking down, but he didn't look as awful as before.

'Better?' said Natasha. Pod nodded.

And that very same evening while Pod was having tea at Natasha's, there was a phone call which Natasha's mummy took out in the hall.

'Marvellous news!' said Natasha's mummy, rushing back into the room with a great big grin on her face. 'Pod, that was your mother on the phone. Your dad's just rung her at work to say he's landed the job he's been after, the one down here, in London! And what's more, Mrs Dovey has agreed to sell him her old house!'

Pod couldn't take it in. He sat there with a chocolate biscuit in one hand and his mouth open. He didn't even blink, he was so surprised.

Natasha's mummy said, 'No-one dared say anything in case it all fell through. Your father's been trying and trying to get a job down here. He kept getting short-listed and not getting the job, but now he has, and you can all be together again. And in your very own house, too!'

Still Pod stared ahead, and didn't speak.

Natasha said 'Wow! What fantastical good news!' She nudged Pod. 'You know another good thing? Your kitten Silver will be able to go back to his old home to live.'

Pod shifted his eyes to Natasha, and back to her mum. He still didn't speak.

'Come, on Pod!' said Natasha. 'Say something!'

Pod put his hands together, closed his eyes, and said, 'Great Pa, ta!'